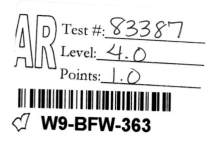

MR. PIN:
The Chocolate Files

ATHENEUM BOOKS BY
MARY ELISE MONSELL

The Mysterious Cases of Mr. Pin
Crackle Creek
Mr. Pin: The Chocolate Files

MR. PIN:
The Chocolate Files

by Mary Elise Monsell
illustrated by Eileen Christelow

Atheneum　　1990　　New York

F
Mon

Atheneum
Macmillan Publishing Company
866 Third Avenue, New York, NY 10022
Collier Macmillan Canada, Inc.
First Edition
Printed in the United States of America

10 9 8 7 6 5 4 3 2 1

Library of Congress Cataloging-in-Publication Data
Monsell, Mary Elise.
Mr. Pin: the chocolate files/by Mary Elise Monsell;
illustrated by Eileen Christelow.—1st ed.   p.   cm.
Summary: Mr. Pin, the rock hopper penguin who has traveled from the
South Pole to be a detective in Chicago, investigates two cases
involving chocolate. Sequel to *The Mysterious Cases of Mr. Pin.*
ISBN 0-689-31639-9
[1. Penguins—Fiction.   2. Chocolate—Fiction.   3. Mystery and
detective stories.]   I. Christelow, Eileen, ill.   II. Title.
PZ7.M7626Mr   1990   [E]—dc20
89-78228   CIP   AC

1301490

With love to Susan and Sarah
—M.E.M.

Contents

MR. PIN:
The Chocolate Files

The Case of the Missing Conductor

1

It was midnight and Chicago was cold. Smiling Sally's diner was closed for the night. But a light was on in the back room. Mr. Pin, famous crime-solving rock hopper penguin, was listening to opera.

Mr. Pin had come from the South Pole to be a detective. He had saved Smiling Sally's from being blown up by ruthless gangsters. Since then, the diner was his home.

The wind blew newspapers down the alley. Mr. Pin put on his checked cap and red muffler and hopped up onto a crate. Then he raised a pencil into the air and pretended to conduct the opera on the radio.

Suddenly, there was a loud *screech* in the alley. It wasn't the wind and it wasn't the opera. The penguin detective dropped his pencil and hopped off his crate.

Quickly, Mr. Pin put out the light and grabbed a heavy rag mop. He was ready for trouble and trouble seemed to be breaking into the back door of the diner.

Just then, the penguin detective smelled something different. Feathers, he thought. But the feathers weren't his. As the back door opened slowly, a feather boa fluttered in the draft. A dark figure stepped inside.

"Stop right there," ordered Mr. Pin. "I have a large mop."

"Please," said a high-pitched voice. "I need your help."

"Help," said Mr. Pin. "Then you'll have to come into my office." With that, Mr. Pin lowered the mop and led the way for the figure in black.

"What's going on?" said Maggie, who appeared in her bathrobe, red hair in all directions. She lived upstairs with her aunt Sally, two gerbils, and a CB radio.

"I'm sorry if it sounded like I was breaking in," said the high voice in the dark. "But I am very famous. I think there might be trouble and I didn't want anyone to see me come here."

Maggie followed the sound of creaking floorboards to Mr. Pin's room. Then she switched on the light.

The dark figure was a lady dressed in a long black coat and pink feather boa. She had thin eyebrows and her lipstick was bright red. "Let me introduce myself," she said. "*I* am Berta Largamente, the opera singer. I think there is going to be a crime at the opera house."

"Crime?" asked Mr. Pin, standing on his typing crate. "What crime are you worried about?"

Maggie sat down on a box of canned tomatoes and took notes. Berta took the only chair, next to the radio, which was still playing opera music.

"I think the conductor is going to be kidnapped," said Berta loudly.

"Kidnapped," said Maggie. "That's serious. Did you call the police?"

"Well, no. I haven't called them yet, but the conductor is acting strangely," explained the opera singer. Then she hurried on, saying, "He's been showing up late. He looks very worried and he's missed my singing cues. I also found a note."

"What about a note? What did it say?" asked Mr. Pin. He turned the radio volume down.

"The note said 'Danger ahead. Watch your step.' " Then to the two detectives, Berta added, "I found it on his music stand."

"On his music stand . . ." repeated Mr. Pin. "The conductor could be in trouble. When can I talk to him?"

"Then you *will* help. I heard you were a famous detective. I wasn't sure you'd take the case." Then Berta added, "You can see him tomorrow night at the opera."

"We'll need tickets," said Mr. Pin.

"Of course," said Berta. "The tickets will be at the box office. You'll have to sit at the top, the very top. The best seats are at the top."

"Why is that?" asked Maggie.

"The sound," said Mr. Pin, "is best at the top."
Screech!

6

"Oh, that's my limousine," said Berta. "I told my driver to go around the block. I need to go. Thank you for your help. I hope you like my solo tomorrow night." Maggie got up to open the back door.

"I was just wondering . . ." Mr. Pin started to say. But Berta didn't hear him and neither did Maggie. Maggie watched the opera star step quickly into the alley, a cloud of pink feathers fluttering behind her. Then Maggie locked up and went upstairs.

"I wonder," said Mr. Pin, this time to himself. "Why didn't Berta call the police?" Then Mr. Pin turned the radio volume up a little. He tapped his pencil on the crate. And as the limousine fishtailed down the alley, Mr. Pin conducted again.

2

It was morning and Mr. Pin was barely awake. But the smell of Smiling Sally's hot cinnamon rolls was too much for the hungry penguin. He put on his red muffler and headed for the steamy diner.

A row of truckers sat at the counter while Smiling Sally poured coffee and served buttery rolls.

"Come on in," she said to each trucker. "Food's good and you meet interesting people."

Mr. Pin sat down at the counter next to Luigi, who drove a pasta truck. Luigi was talking to a well-dressed man who called himself Mac.

"I love opera," said Luigi to Mac. "I always wanted to be an opera singer. Sometimes I sing in my truck when I make pasta deliveries."

"What do you sing?" asked Mac. He was pouring chocolate syrup over his eggs. "By the way, this is great chocolate."

"Tenor," said Luigi. "And thanks. I sell the chocolate to Sally, along with fresh pasta."

"Where do you sing?" asked Mac.

"In my truck," said Luigi.

"We're going to hear the opera tonight," Maggie said

as she came in from the kitchen carrying a tray of cinnamon rolls. "Mr. Pin and I are on a case."

"I'll give you a ride," said Luigi to Maggie and Mr. Pin. "The opera house is on my way to a delivery."

"Thanks," said Maggie. "By the way," she said to Mac, "you're new around here. Where are you from?"

"Italy," said Mac. He looked a little nervous as he quickly put on his coat, paid the bill, and nodded to Smiling Sally.

Mr. Pin picked up the chocolate syrup as he watched Mac leave.

"Who was that?" asked Maggie.

"Mac," said Luigi. "He wants to learn to drive a truck."

"Do you think he's really from Italy?" asked Maggie.

"Yes," said Mr. Pin, pouring syrup directly on the tip of his wing. "But I don't think his name is really Mac."

3

"I always sing when I drive. Keeps me awake," said Luigi to Maggie and Mr. Pin as he drove them to the opera. Luigi sang arias to the music on the radio while Mr. Pin tapped his wing on the dash. Luigi swung his pasta truck behind a long line of limousines parked on North Wacker in front of the opera house. The two detectives climbed out.

"I'll pick you up later," said Luigi.

Mr. Pin and Maggie made their way through the crowd of operagoers to the ticket counter. There they collected their tickets, left by Berta Largamente, and walked over to the elevator.

"Best seats are at the top," the elevator man told Maggie and Mr. Pin when they stepped inside. "I'm Harold. I run this elevator. Matter of fact, I run just about everything else here too."

"I'm Maggie and this is Mr. Pin, penguin detective from the South Pole," Maggie told Harold.

"Reasonable rates," said Mr. Pin.

"Glad to meet you," said Harold as he pulled the door open. The two detectives stepped out. "It's hot," Harold went on, "but the best sound is at the top."

Mr. Pin tipped his cap. Then he and Maggie looked for their seats.

It *was* hot on the upper level. Maggie took off her winter coat. Mr. Pin took a tin of opera chocolates out of a black bag and fanned his feathers. Together they read the program.

Soon the houselights faded. The audience hushed. Tiny flashlights flickered. The curtain parted and there, right in the middle of the stage, was Berta Largamente in a silver sequined gown. The orchestra thundered and Berta started to sing.

Maggie took a pair of binoculars out of her backpack.

"The conductor looks familiar," she whispered. She handed the glasses to Mr. Pin.

"It's Mac," said Mr. Pin. "The same Mac who was in the diner."

"What!" said Maggie, clapping a hand over her mouth.

Suddenly, a dense, blue fog erupted out of the stage floor. It spread everywhere. Berta disappeared almost completely, but she kept singing. Then the blue fog rolled over the edge of the stage and into the orchestra pit. The conductor still held his baton and directed the fog-covered musicians. But all of a sudden, the orchestra stopped playing. The conductor had disappeared!

"Mac is in trouble," said Mr. Pin, springing out of

his seat. Maggie grabbed her backpack and coat and rushed after the penguin detective.

Berta kept singing. The audience was thrilled. They thought the fog was a wonderful special effect.

Mr. Pin raced past the ushers and turned the corner toward the elevators. For some reason, there was an OUT OF ORDER sign on Harold's elevator door. The other two were stopped at the bottom.

"This way," urged Mr. Pin, gently pulling Maggie's elbow toward the stairs.

"Right," said Maggie. They went down six full flights. Then, just as they reached the bottom, the penguin detective stopped short.

"Hmmm," said Mr. Pin, looking around.

"I thought we were in a hurry," panted Maggie.

"We are," said Mr. Pin. "I'm looking for a shortcut from here to the stage."

Quietly, Mr. Pin slipped into the main hall. He motioned for Maggie to follow him. Then he carefully moved his wing along the wall near a fire exit. "Ah. This is it!" he whispered.

"Shhh!" sniffed a lady nearby, not moving her eyes from the stage.

The penguin detective pushed lightly against the wall. A door swung open.

"Amazing," gasped Maggie. "A secret door!" Fortunately, Berta started singing so loudly that the two detectives were able to slip through it unnoticed. Mr. Pin carefully closed the door behind them. Then, down a long, angled hallway, the two raced toward the stage.

"This hallway is called Peacock Alley. Not too many people know about it," said Mr. Pin.

"Just penguins," said Maggie.

After hurrying down Peacock Alley, the two found themselves backstage. Berta had just finished her solo. The curtain closed as the blue fog lifted.

"He's gone!" sobbed Berta as she spotted Maggie and Mr. Pin. "The conductor has been kidnapped."

Mr. Pin offered her a handkerchief from his black bag and asked, "Did you actually see someone take the conductor away?"

"No. But it was just awful," said Berta, blowing her nose. "A part of the stage moved when it wasn't supposed to. Sometimes we move it to make different scenes. Anyway, the stage moved up and a trapdoor opened. After that, the fog came pouring out. The orchestra members couldn't see their music, so they stopped playing. Then no one could see the conductor. That's when he must have been kidnapped. Of course, I kept singing. But they had to close the curtain when I was done. You

can't have an opera without a conductor. Now everyone is out there eating candy and stamping their feet."

"Of course the show must go on," said Mr. Pin. He turned to Maggie. "But first we need to look under the stage . . . for clues."

"Right," said Maggie. "Under the stage."

4

Maggie, Berta, and Mr. Pin walked around the back of the stage and down a few stairs. They entered a dark basement room, directly beneath the stage, filled with hundreds of floor-to-ceiling metal cylinders.

"What are these?" Maggie asked Mr. Pin.

"Hydraulic lifts," said Mr. Pin. "They move the stage up and down." Mr. Pin walked over to one of the cylinders. Nearby was an odd-shaped box. He peered inside.

"Fog machine," said Mr. Pin. "And it's still warm." The detective searched his black bag and took out a small jar of gray powder. Carefully, he dusted the fog machine with a soft brush dipped in powder.

"The thief who took the conductor put the fog machine here. He left fingerprints, but they aren't clear," he added. "There might be more clues in the orchestra pit."

Mr. Pin folded up the fog machine box and tried to lift it. Berta picked up the box and followed the two detectives as they headed for the orchestra pit. They didn't get very far before they met a man with an oboe.

"The conductor is missing!" shouted the man.

"Of course," said Mr. Pin calmly. "He's been kid-napped. I'm on the case."

"I won't sing," said Berta, "without a conductor."

"I understand," said Mr. Pin. Then pointing to the fog machine box, he explained to Maggie, "The police will want to send this to their laboratory."

"Right," said Maggie.

"But no one else can conduct this opera!" insisted the oboe player.

Mr. Pin turned to him and said softly, "Nonsense. I can."

"Miss Largamente to the stage immediately, please," called the stage manager.

Berta looked directly at Mr. Pin and said, "If you conduct, I'll sing."

"If you would," said Mr. Pin to the oboe player. "Direct me to the pit."

"All right," said the oboe player. "But someone needs to make an announcement. Don't you need a tuxedo?"

"Not necessary," was all Mr. Pin said. He picked up his black bag and strode off, conducting himself to the orchestra pit.

It was a little curious for the musicians when Mr. Pin climbed onto the conductor's platform. He needed to have an extra box stacked on top. But strangely enough, no one in the audience seemed to notice that the short black-and-white figure was a penguin about to conduct.

Mr. Pin tapped his music stand and pushed a small

button to signal the stage manager. He raised his baton. The orchestra thundered. The yellow plumes on the side of his head shook. The curtain went up, and, inspired by Mr. Pin, Berta and the chorus sang as they had never sung before.

5

"Bravo! Bravo!" The audience demanded another curtain call. But Mr. Pin, penguin conductor, slipped backstage, his black bag tucked under his wing. Maggie rushed toward him.

"Sally just called. We'll have to take a cab home. She tried using my CB to tell Luigi to pick us up in his truck, but he doesn't answer. And he's not in his pasta shop."

"Hmmmm." said Mr. Pin. "First Mac and then Luigi disappears."

"Do you think they are both kidnapped?" asked Maggie, her eyes growing larger.

"I don't know," said Mr. Pin. "But I do know that chocolate has to be the connection."

"What connection?" asked Maggie.

"Luigi and Mac both like the same chocolate," said Mr. Pin. "Mac was in Smiling Sally's pouring chocolate syrup on his eggs. He was talking to Luigi."

"Do you think Luigi has anything to do with the conductor disappearing?" asked Maggie.

"Maybe," said Mr. Pin. "But I did find something interesting."

"What's that?" asked Maggie.

Mr. Pin opened his black bag and took out a glass bottle of chocolate syrup. "I found this under Mac's music stand," he said. "It's the same chocolate that Smiling Sally uses in her diner. And it is the same syrup that Luigi sells to Sally."

"But how do you know it's from Luigi's pasta shop?" asked Maggie.

"Luigi," explained Mr. Pin, "is the only one I know who sells chocolate in a glass bottle. I think he uses glass so it can be recycled."

"Luigi doesn't sound like much of a kidnapper, does he?" said Maggie.

"No," said Mr. Pin. "But maybe *he* is kidnapped."

"But why," asked Maggie, "would anyone want to kidnap a pasta man who recycles chocolate bottles?"

"I don't know," said Mr. Pin. "But I'm going to find out."

6

It was late when Maggie and Mr. Pin finished talking to the police at the opera house. The officers wrapped a long yellow police tape around the orchestra pit and told the two detectives to go home.

Snow was falling lightly on North Wacker when Mr. Pin and Maggie finally left through the stage door. Mr. Pin stood on the curb and hailed a cab.

"We might have one more clue," said Mr. Pin, as snow covered his checked cap. He searched through his bag as a cab pulled up. He and Maggie stepped inside. The two rode in silence for several blocks until all of a sudden, Mr. Pin held a piece of paper up to his beak and said, "That's it! There's no chocolate!"

"What do you mean there's no chocolate?" asked Maggie. "I thought we were following Luigi's chocolate connection."

"We are," explained Mr. Pin. "But there is no chocolate on this note. And this is the note Berta Largamente found that said 'Danger ahead. Watch your step.'"

Chocolate had been important in most cases, thought Maggie. Not finding chocolate was something new. She wanted to ask Mr. Pin what it meant, but just as they pulled up in front of Smiling Sally's diner, the penguin detective shouted, "Don't stop. Follow that pasta truck."

"Glad to," said the cabdriver, nodding his head. "Been a slow night."

"It's Luigi!" said Mr. Pin to Maggie.

The cab skidded onto Monroe while Luigi's truck raced toward Wabash. The truck squealed around wet corners. But Mr. Pin kept it in sight as it turned west and headed for Greek Town.

"Hurry," said Maggie. "We're after a kidnapper."

"Sure thing, lady," said the cabdriver. His wipers were on full speed as the car crossed the river. But Luigi's truck had disappeared.

"Wait," said Mr. Pin. "Isn't Luigi's pasta shop near here?"

"Just around the corner," said Maggie.

"Turn right," said Mr. Pin to the cabdriver.

Just ahead was Luigi's truck, parked, lights off, in an alley.

"Wait here," said Mr. Pin to the driver. "And keep the change." Mr. Pin handed him a large bill.

"Thanks," said the cabdriver.

"I think we should call the police," said Maggie. But Mr. Pin was already on his way to Luigi's back door. The penguin detective tested the door with his wing. It

was unlocked. There were loud voices inside. Mr. Pin motioned for Maggie to follow him as he slowly opened the door.

But once inside, it wasn't loud talking Mr. Pin heard. It was loud singing. Luigi was singing tenor arias while Mac, the missing conductor, was playing an old upright piano in Luigi's kitchen. Mac stopped abruptly. Luigi looked nervous.

"You're not kidnapped!" shouted Maggie. "But if you're not kidnapped," Maggie asked Mac, "what are you?"

"Missing," said Mac. "On vacation. Not available. Very tired. Not to mention that I always wanted to drive a truck. When Luigi offered to let me deliver pasta, I had to jump for it. The chance might never come again. But it was the middle of the opera season. No one would have let me go. So I had to stage my own disappearance. I called Luigi from the opera house and asked him to pick me up at intermission."

"But the note," said Maggie. "You must have written the note saying you were in danger."

"What note?" asked Mac.

"The note Berta found on your music stand," said Maggie.

"Mac didn't write that note," explained Mr. Pin. "He didn't even see it. Mac had a bottle of chocolate syrup by his music stand. Anyone who likes chocolate that much would have left chocolate stains on a note he had handled. There was no trace of chocolate on the note."

"Then who wrote the note?" asked Maggie.

"Berta Largamente," said Mr. Pin. "My guess is she was really worried about the conductor, his strange behavior, and probably her career. She jumped to the conclusion that Mac might be in trouble or could even be kidnapped. Berta wrote the note to make sure I'd take the case. She never told us why she didn't just call the police."

"How did you know about Luigi?" asked Mac.

"That was simple," Mr. Pin said to Mac. "You had his chocolate nearby when you disappeared and you were seen talking to him in the diner. That's probably when you asked Luigi to help stage your kidnapping. Luigi was probably waiting just outside the opera house in his truck."

"Amazing detective work," said Mac. "I guess I should let people know I'm all right. And I'll need to find someone to take my place while I drive a truck for a little while."

"I think we can work something out," said Mr. Pin, then added, "Just one more thing. I'll bet your name isn't Mac."

"No," said the conductor. "It's not. But Mac sounded more like a truck driver's name. My real name is Alberto Dente."

"But just call him Al," said Luigi, the pasta man.

* * *

Chicago was one of those big cities that made room for a conductor named Alberto Dente who wanted to be a pasta truck driver named Mac for a little while. It also made room for a truck driver, Luigi, who became a star tenor while Mac delivered his pasta. But best of all, the Windy City welcomed a rock hopper penguin detective who conducted the opera for Mac . . . that is, until another case came by Smiling Sally's diner on Monroe.

No reason why big cities can't have big hearts.

A Case of Stolen Eggs

1

Chicago was a hot city in July. Hot streets with cool museums. So when the fans broke in Smiling Sally's diner, Maggie and Mr. Pin went to the Field Museum to look at dinosaurs.

It was bone-dry and cool inside the museum. Spotlights lit huge dinosaur skeletons and exhibits in glass cases. Maggie stopped at the brontosaurus skeleton. Mr. Pin went on to look at protoceratops eggs in a glass case.

Mr. Pin pressed his beak against the glass. Suddenly he noticed a screwdriver glinting in a spotlight. Then a black, gloved hand slowly worked its way up the case. In an instant, the spotlight went out and the whole room was pitch-black.

Alarms howled. Mr. Pin searched in the dark for his black bag. Running feet brushed by. He found his bag and took out a large flashlight. In the flashlight's beam, he caught Maggie crouched next to the great ground sloth. Then he scanned the protoceratops egg case with his light. The black, gloved hand was gone.

Meanwhile, Maggie crept toward Mr. Pin. "It doesn't look like anything is missing," she said.

"Look closely," said Mr. Pin.

"It looks like six protoceratops eggs," said Maggie.

"That's what the thief wanted you to think," said Mr. Pin. "The eggs," he pointed out, "are chocolate."

"Then the real eggs were stolen," said Maggie. "Are there any clues?"

"Chocolate is always a clue," said Mr. Pin.

The glass door of the case had been forced open, so the penguin detective was able to dip his wing into the case and lightly touch a chocolate egg. He preened his wing, then announced, "There is something wrong with this chocolate."

Just then, the lights went on. The air-conditioning hummed again, and a man in a long white coat came running toward Maggie and Mr. Pin.

"What's missing?" asked the man.

"Dinosaur eggs," said Mr. Pin. "The eggs in the case are fake."

"Fake protoceratops eggs. What a tragedy!" said the man, leaning over to study the case.

"Bad chocolate is always a crime," said Mr. Pin.

"We were going to CAT scan the eggs to see what was inside. Museums have been finding unhatched fossil dinosaurs inside fossil eggs."

"Could the dinosaur eggs ever hatch?" asked Maggie.

"Oh, no," returned the man in the white coat. "But the eggs do tell us a lot about what dinosaurs were like.

The CAT scan takes a picture of what's inside the egg, like an X ray."

"You must work for the museum," said Mr. Pin.

"Yes," said the man in white. "I am a paleontologist. I study dinosaurs. I am Professor Hugo Femur."

"I'm Maggie and this is Detective Pin."

"Reasonable rates," said Mr. Pin, tipping his checked cap.

"Glad to meet you," said Professor Femur. He ran his hand through his white hair and tapped his smudged, round glasses. "Looks like we need a detective around here. Do you think you could find the thief who stole the eggs?"

"No problem," said Mr. Pin. "We're on the case."

2

The sky was black. The air was quiet. But a summer storm was about to hit. Maggie and Mr. Pin made it back to Smiling Sally's diner just as rain pelted Monroe Street.

Smiling Sally dished up two pieces of chocolate cream pie as the two detectives walked in.

"Just made it," said Sally, spinning a plate in her hand. "You're the first to try this batch."

Mr. Pin took a large forkful and shoveled it into his beak. First he looked startled. Then he coughed and held his side.

"What's wrong?" asked Maggie.

"Grit," said Mr. Pin. He shook his beak and swayed a little on the diner stool.

"What do you mean 'grit'?" asked Smiling Sally.

But Mr. Pin had trouble talking.

Smiling Sally looked alarmed. "Are you all right?"

"Not all right," gasped Mr. Pin. His eyes clouded and the last thing he managed to say was "Chocolate."

Maggie caught Mr. Pin just before his beak landed in the chocolate cream pie. "I don't understand how he could want more chocolate at a time like this," she said out loud. But it wouldn't be the first time, thought Maggie, that Mr. Pin seemed unusually interested in chocolate.

Smiling Sally helped Maggie carry Mr. Pin to the back room and set him down on the cot.

"It was just a pie. Just a chocolate cream pie," said Smiling Sally.

Maggie took off Mr. Pin's cap and fanned his forehead. After what seemed like an awfully long time, Mr. Pin slowly opened his eyes.

"What happened?" asked Sally, smoothing his feathers.

"Don't eat the chocolate," whispered Mr. Pin. "It's bad."

"Maybe you're allergic to it," suggested Maggie.

"Not possible," snorted Mr. Pin.

"Maybe you've just had too much," said Sally. "After all, it seems like all your cases are solved by eating chocolate."

"I am not allergic to chocolate," insisted Mr. Pin. "This chocolate is bad. It contains grit."

"What do you mean 'grit'?" asked Sally again. "I buy the best chocolate from Luigi."

"Grit is a lot like sand," explained Mr. Pin. "Someone must have known that too much grit can make a penguin sick."

"Oh dear," said Sally.

"I wonder if Luigi had something to do with this," said Maggie.

"It's hard to say," said Mr. Pin, resting his beak on his chest.

"Then I guess now we have two cases to solve," said Maggie. "Valuable dinosaur eggs are replaced by chocolate eggs and somehow Luigi sold Sally some bad chocolate."

"I wonder," said Mr. Pin, holding his side with his wing, "if there is a chocolate problem in this city."

3

Maggie was up early the next morning and poked her head into Mr. Pin's room. Mr. Pin was snoring beneath a large book entitled *Old Bones Picked by New Experts.* Maggie wondered how Mr. Pin had found a fossil book so quickly. But Maggie had other things on her mind.

"I am wondering," said Maggie to the sleeping penguin, "if we should talk to Luigi." Mr. Pin answered with a loud snore.

"We need to find out why Luigi sold bad chocolate to Sally." Mr. Pin barely moved beneath his book.

"Unless, of course," said Maggie a little louder, "you really *are* allergic to chocolate."

"No, absolutely not," said Mr. Pin, opening his eyes and suddenly waking up.

"Sally said she could take us over to Luigi's pasta shop," said Maggie. "Can you go?"

"No problem," said Mr. Pin. He tried sitting up by rocking over to one side. When that didn't work, Mr. Pin tried swinging his feet back and forth. He stayed right where he was. "I don't think I am very well," he said finally. "I am afraid I can't go anywhere."

"But what about the dinosaur eggs?" asked Maggie.

"There is only one thing to do," said Mr. Pin.

"What's that?" asked Maggie.

"You'll have to take the case," said Mr. Pin. "Or the two cases. Go with Sally to Luigi's. Find out as much as you can and try to get a sample of his chocolate."

"Right," said Maggie.

"And one more thing," instructed Mr. Pin.

"What's that?" asked Maggie as she started to leave.

"If you get your CB radio from upstairs," said Mr. Pin to Maggie, "you can set it up next to my bed. That way, we can stay in touch when you go to Luigi's."

"Good idea," said Maggie. "It might save time."

"And time," said Mr. Pin, "is what we need most."

4

Luigi was rolling out fresh pasta when Maggie stepped inside his shop. Sally stayed in her truck and talked to truckers on her CB radio. She called in orders as the truckers made deliveries in Chicago.

"I'm here about your chocolate," said Maggie, hoping to set Luigi off guard.

"Only the best," said Luigi. "I have only the best."

"Have you ever sold a bad batch?" asked Maggie.

"Never. I sell two things," said Luigi. "Pasta and chocolate. Never bad. My chocolate comes straight from Italy."

"I had to ask," said Maggie. "Mr. Pin got sick from the chocolate you delivered to the diner. Now he can't get out of bed and we're on a case of stolen dinosaur eggs."

"You have a case of stolen eggs!" cried Luigi.

"No," said Maggie. "We're looking for stolen eggs."

"I hope you find the case," said Luigi.

"We have the case," said Maggie, "but we're looking for the eggs."

"How can I help?" asked Luigi.

"I need a sample of your chocolate," said Maggie.

"No problem," said Luigi. "I have a case left. In fact, I was saving it for Sally in case she needed it."

"Thanks," said Maggie. "I have a case too." Maggie thought for a minute, then asked, "By the way, has anyone suspicious come into your shop lately?"

"Oh, no," said Luigi. "My customers are the best, only the best. I was just saying that to the fossil man."

"Who?" asked Maggie, getting excited.

"The fossil man," said Luigi. "I buy all of my fossils from him."

"You collect fossils?" asked Maggie.

"Why, yes, I do. In fact," Luigi went on, "the fossil man came into my shop just this week and bought a case of chocolate. I told him he must like chocolate almost as much as Mr. Pin."

"Then what did the fossil man say?" asked Maggie.

"He was very interested in Mr. Pin," said Luigi. "So I told him all about his famous cases. I said Mr. Pin was the best one to call when there was a crime of chocolate."

"Really!" said Maggie. "This is very interesting."

"I hope that helps," said Luigi, wiping flour off his hands. "If you're interested in fossils, I'd be happy to take you over to the fossil shop. It's on my way to a delivery."

"That would be great," said Maggie. "But first, I need to talk to Mr. Pin. Do you have a CB I can use?"

"No problem," said Luigi. "There's one in the kitchen on top of the piano."

5

"Breaker, breaker," said Maggie into Luigi's CB. "This is Orphan Annie at the pasta shop."

"Roger, Maggie," said Mr. Pin from Smiling Sally's. "This is Mr. Pin."

"I have some news," said Maggie. "Luigi collects fossils."

"That sounds suspicious," said Mr. Pin.

"Right," said Maggie. "But he wants to help."

"He may be trying to throw us off the trail," said Mr. Pin.

"Luigi also has a customer who just bought a case of chocolate," said Maggie.

"Who's that?" asked Mr. Pin.

"The fossil man," said Maggie. "Luigi said he'd take me to the fossil man's store if I were interested in fossils."

"You are," said Mr. Pin. "There may be a connection between the fossil man and the stolen dinosaur eggs. But have Luigi meet you there. Tell him you'll get a ride with Smiling Sally. And by the way, did you get the chocolate?"

"Yes," said Maggie. "Luigi said he had a case he was saving for Smiling Sally."

"Good," said Mr. Pin. "Can you bring it by the diner on your way to the fossil shop?"

"We're on our way," said Maggie.

"And one more thing," said Mr. Pin.

"What's that?" asked Maggie.

"Be careful at the fossil shop. It could be trouble. So stall for time. Over and out."

Maggie wasn't sure why Mr. Pin wanted her to stall for time, but he was already off the line. So she hurried back into the front of the pasta shop, where Luigi was putting on a heavy raincoat.

"I'll meet you at the fossil shop," said Maggie to Luigi. "I have to go back to the diner to drop off the case of chocolate."

"So there's a case of chocolate *and* a case of eggs," said Luigi.

"Right," said Maggie. "Two cases."

6

It was raining hard when Sally pulled her truck in front of the diner. Sally kept the motor running while Maggie ran inside with the case of chocolate. Within a few minutes, Maggie came back outside and announced, "Mr. Pin said he would think a lot about chocolate," said Maggie.

"Sounds all right to me," said Sally as she sped away from the curb. Then Maggie read the directions Luigi had given her to the fossil shop.

It was a short ride from the diner. Sally drove her truck next to the river to a dark street underneath Michigan Avenue. Maggie spotted the shop sandwiched between a hot dog parlor and a shoe repair store. It was a small place with fogged windows and a chipped sign: MORT CHISEL'S FOSSIL SHOP—WE BUY AND SELL YOUR VALUABLE FOSSILS.

Sally parked in front of the shop behind Luigi's pasta truck. Sally and Maggie went inside.

The fossil shop was dark and small. There were several glass cases around the walls and one in the center. Behind that was a thin man with a sharp nose and darting eyes. Luigi was in a corner looking at onyx bookends. Sally stood next to Maggie.

"I'm Mort Chisel," said the thin man in a rasping voice. "What can I do for you?"

"I'm Maggie and I'm interested in old bones, preferably fossils."

"Fossils," said Mort, raising an eyebrow almost to his hairline. "How much can you spend?"

"A lot," said Maggie.

"She's starting a collection," said Luigi from the corner.

"I have just the thing," Mort Chisel said quickly. He went through a beaded curtain into a back room.

"Do you think he has a case of eggs?" asked Luigi.

"I don't know," whispered Maggie.

Mort returned shortly, carrying what looked like a large rock.

"Here it is," said Mort with a thin smile.

"I'm sorry," said Maggie. "But this is not a fossil. It's a geode."

"Looks like you know more about fossils than I thought," said Mort. "Would you be interested in a dinosaur egg?"

"Thanks," said Maggie. "It'll look great next to my gerbil cage." Mort went into the back room and returned again, this time carrying what also looked like a large rock. Maggie looked at it carefully, turning it around in her hands.

"Do you have any more?" she asked.

"For a price," said Mort Chisel. "How many do you want?"

Maggie thought quickly. "Six," she said.

Smiling Sally coughed.

"Is that a case?" asked Luigi.

"I have them in the back room if you have enough money."

"Sure," said Maggie, trying to stall.

"Now what are you going to do?" asked Sally.

Just then, a black-and-white figure staggered into the shop. It was Mr. Pin, holding a drenched umbrella with one wing and his side with the other. He leaned against the doorway and said, "I'd like to see those eggs."

"Not a chance," said Mort, starting to back into the beaded curtain.

"That's right," said Mr. Pin. "You don't have a chance of escape. I called the police. The fossil shop is surrounded." Mr. Pin picked up the dinosaur egg Maggie was holding and announced, "This is a protoceratops egg, one of six eggs stolen from the Field Museum."

"Is Luigi in on this?" asked Maggie.

"The chocolate in the eggs at the museum and the chocolate that made me sick are the same," explained Mr. Pin. "It came from Luigi's pasta shop."

"Then Luigi helped Mort steal the dinosaur eggs!" shouted Maggie.

"No," said Mr. Pin. "But Mort wanted you to think that. He framed Luigi. Mort put grit into the chocolate he used to make fake dinosaur eggs. He also slipped grit into the chocolate that went to Smiling Sally's diner. That chocolate ended up in her chocolate cream pie that made me sick."

"Mort did all of that just to make Luigi look guilty?" asked Maggie.

"Right," said Mr. Pin. "And to keep me off the case."

Maggie looked directly at Mort and fumed. "You thought you could keep this fake chocolate egg operation going if you framed Luigi and disabled the only detective in Chicago who could spot your crime. Well, I have news for you, you fake fossil maker. I had you figured the minute I walked in here."

"There's one more thing," said Mr. Pin, coughing slightly. "The case of chocolate you brought by the diner did not contain grit. You said Luigi was saving it for Smiling Sally in case she needed it. If Luigi and Mort were working together, that chocolate would probably have been bad. But it wasn't. In fact, it was quite good, and I am happy to say I have proven that I am not even slightly allergic to chocolate."

"Smart detective work," said Luigi to Maggie and Mr. Pin.

"Great chocolate," said Mr. Pin.

*   *   *

Chicago was a big city, with slick streets when it rained hard. There were plenty of tough cases to solve. But it would take more than a little grit to stop a detective who knew his chocolate as well as he knew his city.

Dear Reader,

Now that you have enjoyed these stories about the incredible Mr. Pin, penguin detective from the South Pole, consider these questions about some of Mr. Pin's previous cases:

1) What flavor ice cream plays an important role in Mr. Pin's efforts to save Smiling Sally's diner from gangsters, in the story "Detective Pin"?

2) What does shrewd Mr. Pin find on the museum wall that leads him to identify the thief in "Mr. Pin and the Picasso Thief"?

3) What kind of pigeon does Mr. Pin use to bait the trap in "Mr. Pin and the Monroe Street Pigeon"?

Hint: All three questions have the same answer, to be found in THE MYSTERIOUS CASES OF MR. PIN, the first book about this clever detective and his sidekick, Maggie.